PAPER CLIP
SCIENCE
Simple & Fun Experiments

Steven W. Moje

Sterling Publishing Co., Inc.
New York

Library of Congress Cataloging-in-Publication Data

Moje, Steven M.
 Paper clip science : simple & fun experiments / Steven W. Moje.
 p. cm.
 Includes index.
 Summary: Describes sixty-five experiments using paper clips and
other inexpensive supplies, demonstrating such basic physics and
chemistry phenomena as weight, balance, flight, and surface tension.
 ISBN 0-8069-4385-8
 1. Science—Experiments—Juvenile literature. 2. Scientific
recreations—Juvenile literature. [1. Science—Experiments.
2. Experiments. 3. Scientific recreations.] I. Title.
 Q164.M575 1996
 530′.078—dc20   96–10993
                                                                            CIP
                                                                            AC

Illustrated by the author; edited by Isabel Stein

10 9 8 7 6 5 4 3 2 1
Published by Sterling Publishing Company, Inc.
387 Park Avenue South, New York, N.Y. 10016
© 1996 by Steven W. Moje
Distributed in Canada by Sterling Publishing
c/o Canadian Manda Group, One Atlantic Avenue, Suite 105
Toronto, Ontario, Canada M6K 3E7
Distributed in Great Britain and Europe by Cassell PLC
Wellington House, 125 Strand, London WC2R 0BB, England
Distributed in Australia by Capricorn Link (Australia) Pty Ltd.
P.O. Box 6651, Baulkham Hills, Business Centre, NSW 2153, Australia

Sterling ISBN 0-8069-4385-8

CONTENTS

TRICKS

Preface

Paper clips are simple, inexpensive, versatile, and can do much more than just hold sheets of paper together. They can be used in many different ways to create fun science experiments. In this book you will learn that paper clips:

- do some surprising (and surprisingly simple) stuff
- take part in amazing balancing acts
- can help objects to fly
- can do wonderful things in water
- engage in electrochemical reactions
- conduct electricity
- are attracted to magnets and can become magnets themselves
- can be made to do tricks!

This book is designed for children in grades 3 to 6, but can be enjoyed by older children as well. Indeed, this book will be fun for all people who have a sense of science adventure in their hearts, including teachers and parents. Text and computer drawings are blended together to create a book that contains 65 easy and fun "hands-on" science experiments.

Types, Sizes, and Shapes of Paper Clips

Paper clips are normally made of metal: steel, which contains iron; copper; or brass. The outside of the paper clip may be coated with a different metal from the one used on the inside—for example, with chrome or copper. With most experiments this will not matter. However, you may discover that similar-looking paper clips behave differently in some of the chemistry, electrochemistry, or magnetism experiments. This different behavior could be due to the different metals within paper clips that look alike.

Paper clips may be plastic-coated. Plastic-coated clips are more colorful and bend more easily than do all-metal paper clips. You should keep in mind that the plastic-coated clips do not work as well in some situations—for example, floating in water, because they are too heavy, or serving as a light switch, because plastic does not conduct electricity.

Paper clips may be made entirely of plastic. For the experiments in this book, use metal paper clips only. The "You will need" list will tell you what kind and size, if a particular kind or size of paper clip is needed. The most common paper clip shape is the "trombone" shape. Trombone-shaped paper clips come in three sizes: small, medium, and large. In the United States, the dimensions of the three common sizes of trombone-shaped paper clips are as follows:

Small Trombone Paper Clip, Standard #3: Normal (bent) dimensions: 1 inch (2.5 cm) long × ¼ inch (.7 cm) wide. Straightened-out length: 3¼ inches (8 cm)

Medium-Sized Trombone Paper Clip, Standard #1:
Normal (bent) dimensions: 1⅜ inches (3.5 cm) long
× ⁷⁄₁₆ inch (.8 cm) wide. Straightened-out length:
4 inches (10 cm)

Large (Jumbo) Trombone Paper Clip: Normal (bent)
dimensions: 2 inches (5 cm) long × ⁷⁄₁₆ inches
(1.1 cm) wide. Straightened-out length = 6¼ inches
(15.9 cm)

If you do not have exactly these sizes, use paper
clips that are close in size.

Sometimes you will need to bend or straighten
paper clips in order to do science experiments with
them. The parts of a paper clip that may be bent or
straightened are called the loops and the ends (see
figure). There are three loops (inner, middle, and
outer) and two ends (the inside and outside end).

There are two special types of paper clips that do
not have the traditional trombone shape: the double-
prong and the butterfly (or clamp).

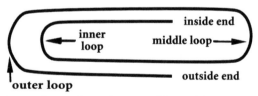

A trombone-shaped paper clip and its parts.

The double-prong clip is not much larger than the
#3 trombone paper clip. It is useful whenever you
need to have one or two small circular loops—for
example, when you make soap bubbles.

The butterfly clip (also called a butterfly clamp) is

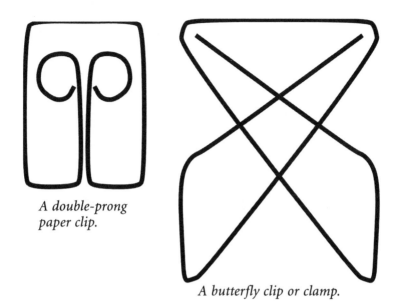

A double-prong paper clip.

A butterfly clip or clamp.

normally larger than the traditional trombone-shaped paper clip. It is called a butterfly clip because it is shaped like butterfly wings. It is useful whenever you need a paper clip larger than the largest (jumbo) trombone clip.

Now you're ready to do some paper clip science. Choose an experiment you are interested in and look at the "You will need" list. Assemble your materials and get ready for some fun.

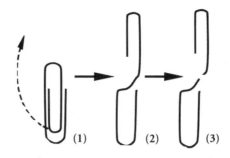

(1)   (2)   (3)

SIMPLE PROPERTIES
Tired Paper Clip (Metal Fatigue)

You will need: trombone paper clips of different sizes, including a plastic-coated paper clip

Pull the inner loop of a paper clip up and away from the outer loop, as shown in part 2 of the figure. Holding the two loops, bend the paper clip at the center until the clip breaks (this will take about 20 to 30 bends). The metal breaks because repeated bending weakens the forces that hold the metal together. This is called "metal fatigue." Try bending different sizes of paper clips. Does a small paper clip break more quickly than a large paper clip? If you touch the center of the paper clip to your wrist before the clip breaks, you will feel that the center gets warm as you twist the loop back and forth. The heat comes from the metal atoms rubbing against each other, in the same way that your hands will get warm if you rub them together.

On the other hand, when you try to break apart a plastic-coated metal paper clip, it will stay together even after the metal core has broken, because plastic is more pliable (less brittle) than metal.

I'm Not Moving! (Inertia)

You will need: paper clip, plastic cup or tumbler, 3 × 5 inch (7.6 × 12.7 cm) index card or strip of notebook paper

A paper clip will stay put if the surface on which it is resting is pulled (or pushed) away quickly enough. This "staying put," the tendency of an object to remain wherever it is located, is called *inertia*.

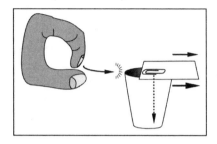

With an index card: Place the index card on top of the tumbler or cup. Put the paper clip in the center of the card and put the card over the center of the tumbler or cup. Knock the card away by flicking it with your finger and thumb. As the card flies off, the paper clip will drop right into the cup.

With a piece of notebook paper: Place the paper just as you placed the card, and put the paper clip on top of it. If you pull the paper strip slowly, the paper clip will be pulled off the cup onto the table. To make the paper clip fall into the cup, try one of the following:

1. Tape a piece of string or thread to the paper. Give the paper a swift tug. The paper clip should drop right into the cup; or

2. Hold the loose end of the paper strip with one hand. Holding a ruler in your other hand, quickly strike the paper (downward) with the ruler. The paper will be jerked away, and the paper clip will fall right down into the cup!

Paper Clip Rulers (Length Measurement)

You will need: 10 to 60 medium-sized trombone paper clips; objects to measure

Connect 10 to 60 paper clips in a chain, as shown in the figure. To measure a small object (a pencil, for example) use a short chain (about 10 paper clips long). To measure a large object (for example, a chair), use a chain 40 to 60 paper clips long. There is no "best" size of paper clip, but make sure that all the paper clips in that chain are the same size.

 chain

Measure how long, wide, and deep certain objects are. How about your favorite book? The dining room table? Your arm? Your little finger? The distance between your big and little toes? The length and width of a pocket calculator? Notebook paper? Have fun measuring!

side by side

Another way to use paper clips for measurement is to turn them sideways. How many paper clips turned sideways and placed next to each other does it take to equal the length of 10 paper clips linked together?

Paper Clip Scale (Weight Measurement)

You will need:
1 inch × 12 inch (2.5 cm × 30 cm) piece of foam-core board, heavy corrugated cardboard the same size, or a coat hanger; two paper cups; thread or string; clay; a ballpoint pen; many paper clips; ruler; scissors

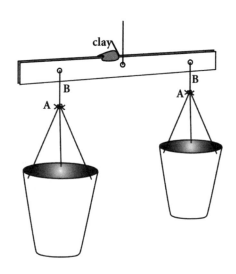

Let's make a scale to weigh things! Punch three holes in the rims of two paper cups; use a ballpoint pen to easily and safely make these holes. The holes should be at equal distances apart from each other. Put a knot in one end of each of six pieces of string that are about 4 inches (10 cm) long, and push the unknotted end of each string through a hole in a cup, working from inside the cup outwards. About 3 inches (7 cm) above each cup, tie the three ends of the string from that cup together as shown in the figure.

Take the 1 × 12 inch piece of foam-core board or cardboard.* Punch three holes through the board: one

---

*If you do not have any foam-core board or cardboard, you can use a coat hanger instead.

in the center, and one an inch (2.5 cm) in from each end of the board. Tie a piece of string through the center hole. Hang the board from the edge of a table by tying the center string around something heavy, such as a large piece of wood. Tie a string about 10 inches (25 cm) long from each of the two side holes (*B* in the figure) to the knot of three strings (*A*) attached to each cup (*A*). Place a piece of clay near the center support of the board, and move the clay until the board is level (both sides are in balance).

Weighing fun: try putting a small object (pencil, rock, gumball, candy, envelope, coin, eraser) in one of the cups. Place paper clips in the other cup until the two cups balance. How many paper clips does it take to balance each object? The units of measurement may be called paper-clip units (pcu's).

Rubber Band Ruler Scale (Weight Measurement)

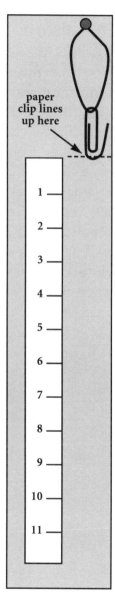

You will need: piece of foam-core board or corrugated cardboard, ruler, rubber band, paper clips, paper fastener or thumbtack, glue or tape, scissors, small objects to weigh

Glue or tape a 12-inch ruler (or a 30-cm ruler) to a piece of 20 × 4 inch (51 × 10 cm) foam-core board or corrugated cardboard. Leave about 4 to 6 inches (10 to 15 cm) at the top of the board as shown. Bend the outside end of a paper clip to make a hook. Hang the paper clip on a rubber band and press the thumbtack or paper fastener into the top right-hand corner of the board, so that the paper clip hook is lined up with what would be the zero (0) on the ruler. (If you use a paper fastener, push it through the board and open its "feet" out on the other side of the board to hold it.)

Place the board in an upright (vertical) position by gluing or taping it to a wall or door. Attach small objects (such as various types, sizes, and numbers of paper clips) to the paper clip hook to see how much they weigh. The further down the ruler the paper clip hook is pulled, the heavier the object is.

Read "weight" measurements from the the inch or centimeter markings on the ruler. The heavier the object, the higher the number on the ruler. How many paper clips do you need to add to cause your paper clip hook to drop down one inch? To drop down two inches? To drop down three inches? (Etc.) Does it take the same number of paper clips to cause the paper clip hook to move down a half-inch (or a centimeter) at any point on the scale? For example, is a greater number of paper clips needed to move the hook from 1 inch to 1½ inches than from 0 inches to ½ inch? (Is a greater number need to move the hook from 2.5 cm to 3.5 cm than is needed to move it from 0 cm to 1 cm?)

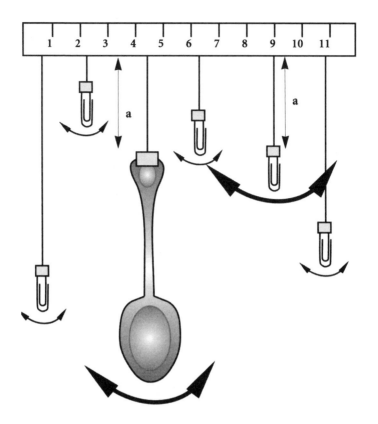

A Swingin' Good Time
(Momentum Transfer)

You will need: ruler, sewing thread or string, 5 paper clips, a spoon, tape, scissors.

Cut some thread or string into six pieces. Make two of the pieces the same length (*a* in the figure); the other pieces should be of different lengths. Tape or tie a paper clip to each piece of thread, saving one of the *a* pieces (equal-length pieces) to tape or tie to a spoon. Tape or tie all of the threads to different points on a ruler.

Hold the ruler horizontally and start swinging the spoon. You will notice that although all the paper clips will start swinging, the paper clip that is attached to the thread of length a will at first swing with lots of energy and then slow down as the spoon, which also is attached to a thread of length a, swings more vigorously.

The paper clip on the string of length a is affected more strongly than the other paper clips because the motion set up by the spoon is most easily transferred to an object that is hanging by an identical length of thread. The vibration of the strings is in the form of waves. And for any two strings to vibrate in harmony with each other, the wavelengths must be the same. You may have noticed that if you pluck a guitar, let the sound die out, and then hum the same note, the guitar string will make a soft sound even after you are no longer playing it. This is because your voice is sending out a sound wave whose length is the same as the guitar string's wavelength.

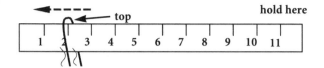

Walking Paper Clips (Hand Steadiness)

You will need: ruler, trombone paper clips

Straighten out a paper clip. Bend it at the center in the shape of a *U* or a *V*. Try to smooth out all the bumps, except for the bend at the center. Place the paper clip on the edge of a ruler; a tableware knife will also work. Pick up the ruler and the paper clip straddling it and lower the ruler gently toward a smooth table top, until the paper clip "feet" just barely touch the table.

Try as hard as you can to hold the paper clip steady. You will not be able to! Instead of staying in one place, the little feet of the paper clip will "walk" along the top edge of the ruler! To make the trick work best, do not rest your hand or arm or elbow on the table or anything else. If the top of the U or *V* is pointed toward you, the clip walks toward you. If the *V* is pointed away from you, the clip will walk away from you.

Try putting several paper clips on the ruler at the same time. To make the paper clips walk away from you, tilt *up* the end of the ruler which you are holding. To make the paper clips walk toward you, tilt the ruler *down,* towards you. Try really hard to hold the ruler steady. The paper clips will only walk faster! The paper clips move because the muscles in your arm are constantly expanding and contracting.

19

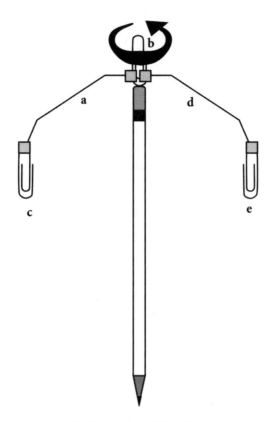

BALANCING

Paper Clip Balancer/ Spinner

You will need: 5 trombone paper clips (of equal size), tape, pencil (optional)

Straighten out two paper clips to make two wires (*a* and *d* on the figure). Tape the end of the *a* wire to the side of unstraightened paper clip *b*, just above the end loop (see figure). Tape the second of the wires *(d)* to the center paper clip *(b)*. Tape two more paper clips (*c* and *e)* to the free ends of wires *a* and *d* as shown.

Balance the end of the center paper clip *(b)* on a pencil or on your finger. If you hold the pencil steady enough, you can even spin the paper clip around on it!

This experiment, and other balancing experiments like it, works because the center of gravity is *below* the location of the balance point. The center of gravity is the point at which the paper clip balancer has its weight distributed evenly. This is an invisible point, lying below the upper (central) clip and above the two lower clips. When you try to raise either "arm" of the balancer, the center of gravity is raised also, and tries to return to its original (lower) spot.

Paper Clip and Pipe Cleaner Balancer/Spinner

You will need: 3 equal-sized trombone paper clips, 2 long pipe cleaners, pencil (optional)

Push one end of a pipe cleaner between the wires about halfway up one side of a paper clip and twist it around the clip to fasten it. Do the same on the other side. The long pipe cleaner ends should stick out from this paper clip at about 45-degree angles. Twist the other end of each pipe cleaner around the end of one of the other two paper clips.

Balance the middle paper clip on your finger or on the end of a pencil eraser. Give the paper clip and pipe cleaner balancer a gentle push and watch it spin around!

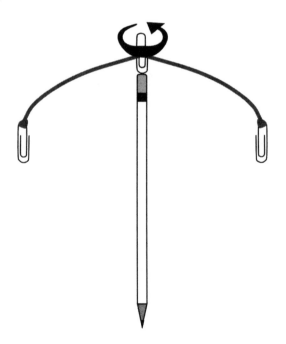

Rocking Pencil

You will need: a jumbo trombone paper clip and a pencil or crayon

Unbend, but do not completely straighten out, the inner, middle, and outer loops of a jumbo trombone paper clip. The paper clip wire should have a 90-degree (right-angle) bend near each end, and the center bend should be nearly straightened out (see figure).

Stick one end of the paper clip wire into the eraser end of a pencil. Put the other end of the paper clip on your finger. Rock the pencil back and forth gently. The pencil will not fall off!

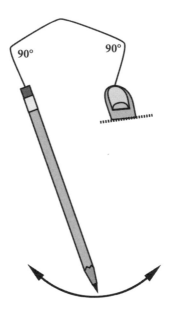

Square Balances Circle

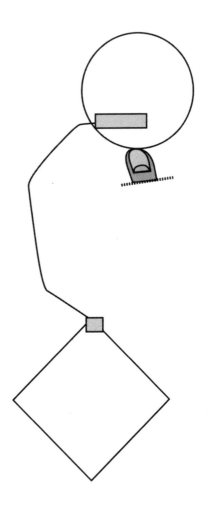

You will need: jumbo trombone paper clip, tape, 5 × 8 inch (12.7 × 20 cm) index card or other stiff card, compass (optional)

Cut out a 3-inch (7.5 cm) circle from one end of the index card. If you don't have a compass, trace a circle from the bottom of a cup or can. Cut out a 5-inch square from the other end of the card. Unbend a jumbo paper clip as shown in the figure. Tape one end of the paper clip wire to the edge of the circle and the other end to a corner of the square. Place the edge of the circle on your finger. The circle will balance the square! Try this experiment with other shapes.

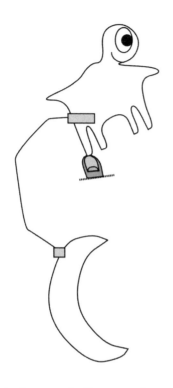

Martian Cow-Critter Jumps over the Moon

You will need: jumbo trombone paper clip, tape, two 4 × 6 inch (10 × 15 cm) index cards or pieces of cardboard, scissors, tracing paper, pencil, glue. (The patterns are on page 26.)

Trace out a Martian cow-critter and glue it to one of the index cards. Draw a face on the cow. Cut out the cow. Trace a crescent-shaped moon and glue it to the other index card. Cut out the moon.

Unbend a jumbo paper clip as shown. Tape one end to the lower rear of the cow-critter and other end to the top edge of the moon.

Place the cow-critter's hind leg on your finger. It will balance on its leg and not fall off!

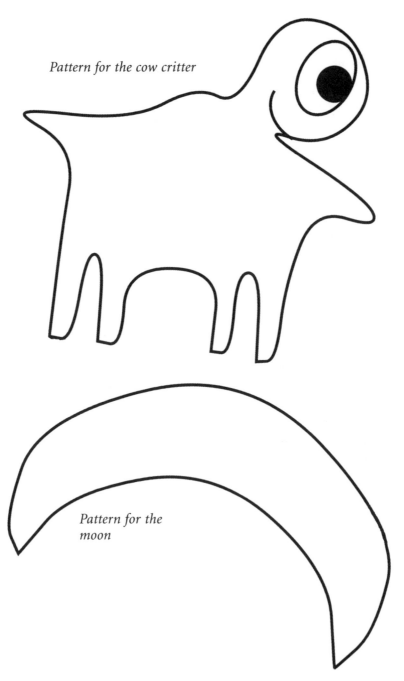

Pattern for the cow critter

Pattern for the moon

Balancing, Bouncing, Flapping Bird

You will need: 4 jumbo trombone paper clips, 5 × 8 inch (12.7 × 20.3 cm) index card or similar cardboard, pencil or crayon, scissors, glue, tracing paper

Trace the pattern on the next page and paste it onto the index card or cardboard. Then cut out the bird from the index card or cardboard.

If you draw the bird freehand, you can make sure that the wings are identical by folding the index card in half to make a 4 × 5 inch (10 × 12.7 cm) folded card. Draw the right or left-hand side of the bird on the card, and then cut out the whole bird with scissors through the folded card. Make sure that the beak of the bird is on the fold and not on the edge of the index card. Unfold the bird.

Draw a beak and eyes on the bird. Link two paper clips together. Clip or tape them on the end of one of the wings. Repeat with two more paper clips on the end of the other wing.

Balance the bird on your fingertip by its beak. Watch the bird's wings bounce and flap as you move your finger up and down!

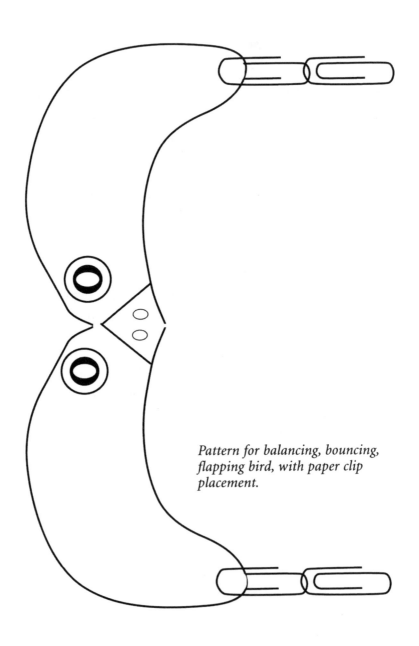

Pattern for balancing, bouncing, flapping bird, with paper clip placement.

Balancing Belt Hook

You will need: jumbo trombone paper clip, belt

Bend a jumbo paper clip into the shape shown. Slide a belt through the loop. You will be able to balance the belt and paper clip on the end of your finger! If you take the belt away, the paper clip will fall off your finger.

FLYING THINGS
Spinning Clipsplate

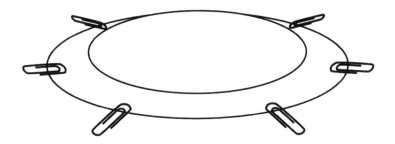

You will need: 4 to 8 jumbo trombone paper clips; paper, plastic or Styrofoam plate; tape; scissors

Cut off the raised edge from a paper, Styrofoam, or plastic plate. The resulting disk should be nearly, but not completely, flat. Place paper clips around the edge of the disk, at equal distances from each other. Tape the paper clips onto the disk so that they do not fly off.

Throw the spinning clipsplate in the same way that you would throw a store-bought plastic flying saucer. Does the clipsplate fly better with the bottom-side up or with the bottom-side down?

Try using 4, 6, 8, or even more paper clips for your experiment. Which combination works the best? Does the disk fly straighter or longer with more paper clips or with fewer?

Plate Planes

You will need: about 10 medium trombone paper clips, paper plates and Styrofoam plates, glue, scissors, pencil, tracing paper

Planes can be cut out of either paper plates or Styrofoam plates in a variety of shapes (see the patterns on the next page). A good-flying plane has: *light weight, balance* between the left and right hand sides, *rigidity* (stiffness), an *airfoil* (curve in the tail end), which gives at least a little bit of lift, and one or more *paper clips* attached to the nose. The weight of the clips balances the lift caused by the tail; without clips, the plane flies nose up and stalls. Styrofoam plates—which are stiffer, yet lighter, than paper plates—become better-flying airplanes than paper plates do. Since paper plates are cheaper, practice cutting your design out of paper first. Trace out and enlarge a pattern and glue it to a paper plate. Use the outside rim of the paper plate for the tail. Cut out the plane through both layers. After you try your design out and are satisfied, cut the final version out of Styrofoam. Put clips on as shown.

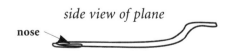

side view of plane

nose

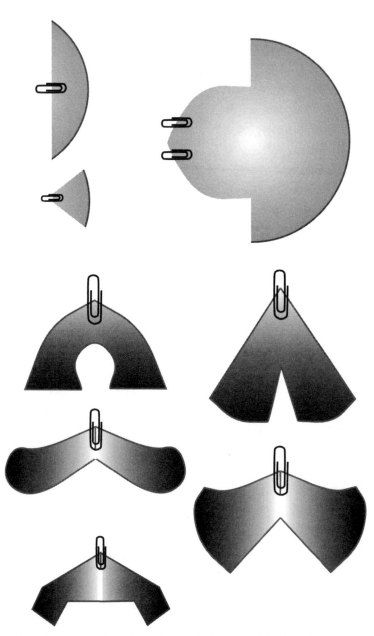

Reduced patterns for plate planes. Enlarge to 160% or larger.

Tube-y Straw Clip Glider

You will need: 2 medium-sized (standard #1) trombone paper clips; 1 drinking straw; stiff paper, such as construction paper; tape; scissors; ruler

Cut the paper into two strips: one 7 inches × 1 inch (18 cm × 2.5 cm) and the other 7 inches × ¾ inch (18 cm × 2 cm). Bend each strip into a loop and fasten it with a paper clip. Attach each loop with its paper clip to one end of the straw; see figure.

Make sure that the loops are lined up; when you look down the straw through one of the loops, the other loop should be centered in it.

You may adjust the size of either loop by pushing or pulling the strip of paper through the paper clip. Fly your glider by throwing it into the air ahead of you. After you are satisfied with how your glider flies, tape the paper clips in place so they don't move.

Straw Clip Propeller

You will need: small trombone paper clip; drinking straw; 3 × 5 or 4 × 6 inch (7.5 × 13 cm or 10 × 15 cm) index card or some other piece of thin cardboard; scissors

Cut a piece about ½ inch (1 cm) wide and 5 inches (13 cm) long from an index card. Fasten the paper clip to the middle of the index card piece. Give each end of the card a twist or bend (in opposite directions), near the paper clip.

Stick the paper clip end into one end of a drinking straw (see figure). Hold the straw between both hands. Give it a spin. The propeller should fly several feet up into the air. If the propeller flies downward instead of upward, give it a spin in the opposite direction with your hands. If the propeller does not fly, try adjusting the "twist" of the propeller. Make sure that you've given both sides an equal twist. Also make sure that the paper clip/cardboard piece is not lopsided; there must be an equal amount of paper on both the right- and left-hand sides of the propeller.

Silly Spinning Split Clip Cards

You will need: 2 to 4 trombone paper clips of different sizes; three 3 × 5 inch (7.6 × 12.7 cm) index cards or construction paper cut to this size; crayons; scissors; ruler

Cut partway down the middle of a 3-inch (7.5 cm) side of a 3 × 5 inch index card, about 4 inches (10 cm) into the card, leaving 1 inch (2.5 cm) uncut (see figure *a*). Bend one of the cut sides away from you, and the other side toward you (figure *b*). Slide one or more paper clips onto the center of the uncut portion of the card; try different sizes. You've made a silly spinning split clip card!

Make another silly spinning split clip card, but this time bend the sides in directions *opposite* to the way you bent them for the first card (figure *c*). Drop each of the split clip cards. They will spin in opposite

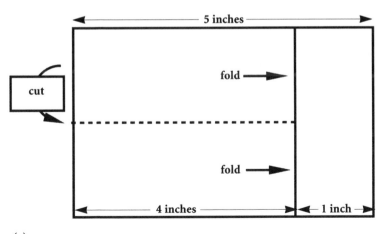

(a)

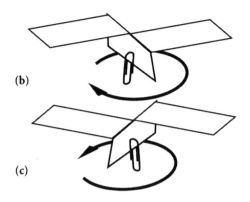

(b)

(c)

directions. This is because the cards are mirror images of each other. When you reflect something in a mirror, all its parts are reversed (as the letters in this book are, when it is held up to a mirror). In a similar sense, air flows in opposite directions around two mirror image objects. The card that has the left flap bent *toward* you and the right flap bent away from you will spin clockwise. The other card (left flap *away* from you, right flap *toward* you) will spin in the opposite direction (counterclockwise).

Extra fun: Put a little water on one wing of one of the silly spinning split clip cards. Does it help the rotation, or does it cause the card to behave strangely? Cut the card along the short (3-inch) axis, rather than the long (5-inch) axis. Does the spinner work better or worse? Use crayons to color patterns on the cards. Watch what happens to the colors while the cards spin.

Paper Clip Paper Helicopter

You will need: one small trombone paper clip; one piece of 8½ × 11 inch (22 × 28 cm) notebook paper; ruler; pencil; scissors

You can make FOUR helicopters from just one piece of notebook paper! Fold the top edge of a piece of notebook paper to meet the bottom edge, so its folded size is 5½ × 8½ inches (14 × 22 cm). Fold it in half again, the same way, so its folded size is 2¾ × 8½ inches (7 × 22 cm). Open out the paper and cut it along the folds. This will give you four pieces of paper, each 2¾ × 8½ inches (7 × 22 cm).

From one of the 2¾-inch (7 cm) edges of a strip, cut about 3½ inches (9 cm) down the center. The two flaps that result (*A* in figure 1) will be the blades of

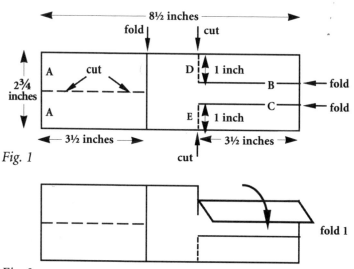

Fig. 1

Fig. 2

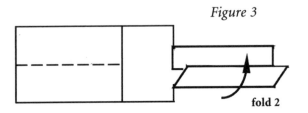

Figure 3

fold 2

the helicopter. On the other 2¾-inch side, mark off an
inch (2.5 cm) in from each long side. Rule 3½-inch
lines (*B* and *C* in
figure 1) starting
from the inch
marks, parallel to
the long sides of
the paper. Rule *D*
and *E*, each 1 inch
(2.5 cm) long, as
shown in figure 1,
and cut along *D*
and *E*. Fold the
first side piece

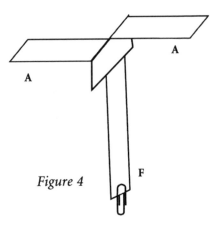

Figure 4

along *B* so it overlaps the center part of the paper (see
figure 2). Fold the other side piece along *C* so it overlaps the first piece (see figure 3). Place a paper clip at
F as shown in figure 4.

Fold the *A* flaps, one toward you and the other
away from you, as shown in figure 4. Drop your
helicopter and watch it spin!

WATER FUN
Disappearing Paper Clip

You will need: one trombone paper clip, clear drinking glass, water

Place a paper clip *beneath* an empty clear drinking glass. Look at the paper clip at a low angle through the glass.

Pour water into the glass so it is about one-fifth full. The paper clip will seem to have disappeared!

The reason for the "disappearance" is that when you add water to the glass, the light rays from the paper clip travel in a different direction. When the light rays hit the bottom of the water surface, they are reflected away from your sight, and the paper clip seems to have disappeared!

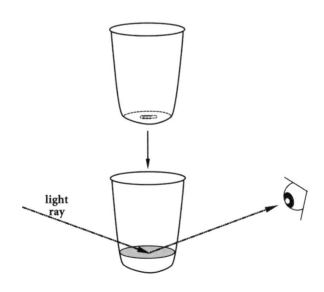

light
ray

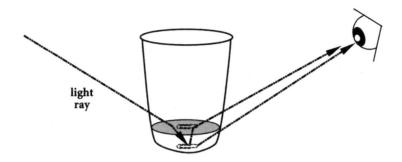

light
ray

Extra Paper Clip

You will need: one paper clip; clear drinking glass;
water

Place a paper clip in the bottom of an empty
drinking glass. Pour water into the glass so it is about
one-fifth full.

Look at the paper clip at a medium angle through
the glass. Now you will see not just one, but two,
paper clips: one on the bottom of the glass, and the
other one apparently floating on the surface of the
water! This is an optical illusion. It is caused by light
rays travelling at different angles in air and in water.
One paper clip gives *two* images!

It is interesting that when you put the paper clip
inside the drinking glass, you see TWO paper clips.
And when you put the paper clip *underneath* the
drinking glass (see the Disappearing Paper Clip
experiment), you see NO paper clip!

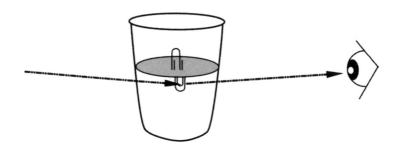

"Broken" Paper Clip

You will need: one paper clip; clear drinking glass; water.

Lower a paper clip into a glass of water. Look at the glass directly from the side. The paper clip will seem to be cut in two, with its upper and lower parts not connected.

The reason for this is that light rays are bent at different angles in water and in air. Consequently, the light rays travel different paths to reach your eyes. Your eyes "tell" you that the paper clip is no longer in one piece!

Race to the Bottom
(Air vs. Water Resistance)

You will need: 4 trombone paper clips, clear drinking glass, water, piece of aluminum foil 1 × 1 inch (2.5 × 2.5 cm)

Drop a paper clip into an empty clear drinking glass. Notice how quickly the clip falls to the bottom. Now fill the glass with water. Drop the paper clip into the glass again. The paper clip takes longer to reach the bottom of the glass. Water slows down the paper clip more than air does. This is because water has greater resistance to an object than air does. In addition, a paper clip falls straight to the bottom in air, whereas in water the paper clip may flip-flop or wobble as it drops.

Another experiment: In water, will the paper clip fall most slowly when dropped: *(A)* with the loop end pointed down; *(B)* with the edge pointed down; or *(C)* with the flat side parallel to the water?

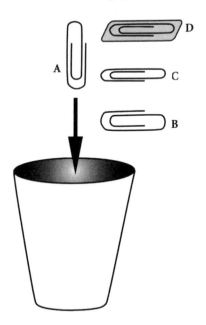

You will discover that paper clip *C* takes a little longer to reach the bottom than *A* or *B*, because a paper clip dropped flat onto the surface of the water has more resistance to going through the water. The water is pressing on more paper clip surface area than it did when *A* dropped nose-first or *B* dropped edge-first.

Next, wrap a paper clip in aluminum foil *(D)*, and drop it into the water. It will probably float, because of the air trapped in the foil. Squeeze the foil to release the trapped air, and drop it in the water again. The foil-covered paper clip will sink, but not as fast as the paper clips that were not foil-covered. The foil gives even more surface area for water to push against. As a result, a foil-covered clip *(D)* falls more slowly than clips *A, B,* or *C*.

Rising Rim

You will need: 40 to 80 paper clips; a clear drinking glass; water

Completely and carefully fill a drinking glass with water. Slowly and gently drop paper clips into the water. While adding the paper clips, look at the rim of the glass from the side. You will see that the water level will rise above the rim as you add the paper clips. This is because water has a property called *surface tension,* the tendency of a liquid to want to hold itself together.

Water has a thin "skin," which bulges above the top of the drinking glass when paper clips are added. After the water level gets so high that it cannot hold itself together any longer, it spills over the top of the glass.

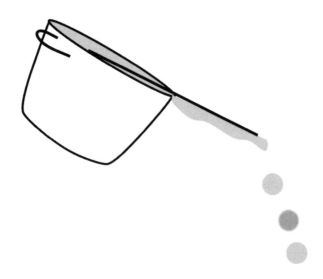

Water Pours Sideways

You will need: large (jumbo) trombone paper clip; a small paper cup, about 3 ounces (90 mL); water

Unbend a large paper clip, but leave a hook at the end. Push the partially unbent paper clip end through one side of a small paper cup, one-eighth inch (.3 cm) down from the rim. Lay the straight end of the paper clip on the opposite side of the rim of the cup. Add water to the cup until it is nearly full.

Tip the cup so that the long end of the paper clip is pointed sideways and down. Watch the water flow sideways down the paper clip! Water runs down the paper clip and not straight down toward the ground because of the *surface tension* of the water (the tendency of water molecules to stick together).

Magic Floating Paper Clip

You will need: two trombone paper clips; bowl of water; soap

Unbend one of the paper clips to make a "cradle" to hold the other paper clip (see figure). Use the cradle to lower a second paper clip gently, slowly (and straight down) into a bowl of water. If you do it carefully enough, the paper clip will float!

Look closely, and you will see that the surface of the water that is holding up the floating paper clip is "bent" by the weight of the paper clip pressing down into the "skin" of the water. The water, because of its surface tension, holds up the paper clip. To break the surface tension, just add a piece of soap or a drop of detergent to the bowl of water. Watch the paper clip fall to the bottom of the bowl!

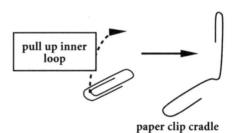

pull up inner loop

paper clip cradle

Paper Clip Foil Boat

You will need: 5 to 15 paper clips; piece of aluminum foil about 6 × 6 inches (15 × 15 cm) to 9 × 9 inches (22 × 22 cm); bowl of water

Shape the aluminum foil into a boat and place it on the water. Add at least 5 paper clips to it. The boat should continue to float.

Take the boat out of the water. Wad the foil boat over the paper clips by crunching it up. Put it back in the bowl of water. If you have squeezed out all of the air bubbles, the boat will sink.

Reason: when the foil was in the shape of a boat, it displaced a volume of water that was equal to the weight of the paper clips. After you wadded up the foil (with the paper clips in it), you lost the boat's shape. Then the boat could not displace its weight in water, and the boatload of paper clips consequently could not stay afloat.

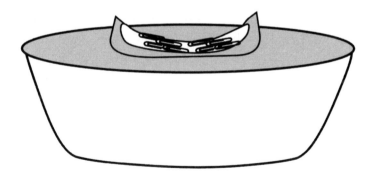

Paper Clip Water-Drop Magnifier

You will need: trombone paper clip or double-prong paper clip, bowl of water, needle-nosed pliers,* piece of newspaper

Make a paper-clip cradle as shown in the Magic Floating Paper Clip experiment. With a needle-nosed pliers, bend the inner loop of the paper clip cradle into a circular loop ⅛ to ½ inch (.3 cm to 1.2 cm) in diameter. Try to make the tiny loop as round as possible.

Dip the loop end into the bowl of water; the water film across the loop will act as a magnifier. Hold your magnifier over some small print on the newspaper, and watch it magnify! (The smaller the loop, the longer the drop will last.)

cradle

Double-prong paper clips have ready-made circular loops. Simply unbend the paper clip. One loop holds your water droplet, and the other loop is your handle.

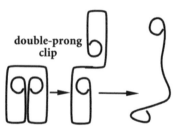

double-prong clip

---

*A needle-nosed pliers has long, pointy jaws to hold small things. If you don't have one, use regular pliers.

Paper Clip Bubble Wand

You will need: three trombone paper clips (two medium and one large); a double-prong clip; and a butterfly clip; dishwashing liquid; water; pipe cleaner

Trombone paper clips (medium and large): Bend one end of the paper clip into a loop ½ to 1 inch wide (1.2 to 2.5 cm). It does not matter if the loop is round, but make sure that the wire end touches the rest of the paper clip; otherwise, bubbles will not form. The medium-sized paper clip will give a steadier (longer) stream of bubbles.

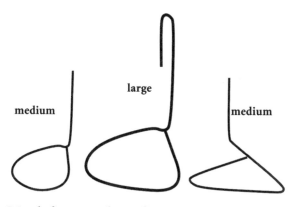

Wands from trombone clips.

Double-prong clip: Bend the two circular loops apart, as shown in the Water Drop Magnifier experiment. Either circular end will make very small bubbles. Use the other end as the handle.

Butterfly clip: Make a large bubble wand by bending down one-half of a butterfly paper clip at a 90-degree angle (see figure). Use the larger "loop" to dip into the bubble solution. The other part is the handle.

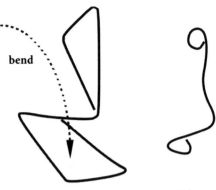

bend

Wand from butterfly clip.

Wand from double-prong clip.

Bubble solution: Mix 1 part dishwashing liquid to 10 parts water. Put your bubble solution in a small (3 ounce or 90 mL) paper cup.

Dip the bubble wand into the solution. Lift it out and blow bubbles! Wrap a pipe cleaner around the loop to give even longer-lasting bubbles.

Straw Triangle Bubble Wand

You will need: 6 medium-sized trombone paper clips, 3 drinking straws, duct tape or other waterproof tape; dishwashing liquid; water

Hook two paper clips together at their outer-loop ends. Repeat the process with two more sets of paper clips. You will now have three sets of paired paper clips. These will be your connectors.

duct tape the corners

Push the unjoined (inner loop) end of each of the paired clips into a straw. Repeat the process until you have linked together three straws in the shape of a triangle (see figure). To keep the paper clips from slipping, tape the corners of the triangle with waterproof tape.

Dip the triangle into a plate or bowl of bubble liquid (1 part dishwashing liquid in 10 parts of water). Pull the triangle out of the liquid and blow large bubbles with it. You also can make other shapes from straws and paper clips–for example, squares.

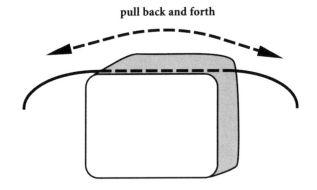

pull back and forth

Slicing the Ice with a Paper Clip

You will need: medium-sized (standard #1) trombone
paper clip, cold ice cube, dinnerplate

Unbend a paper clip. Lay it across an ice cube that
just has been taken out of the freezer.

Pull the unbent paper clip back and forth across the
surface of the ice cube, applying pressure as you do so.
The wire of the paper clip will move into the ice cube,
cutting it.

After about a minute, you'll be able to raise the ice
cube by lifting the paper clip. The water above where
the paper clip is cutting has now had a chance to
refreeze, and locks the paper clip to the ice cube.

Do not use an ice cube that has been sitting out at
room temperature too long, since it will not be able to
refreeze the melted water above the paper clip, because
it is too warm.

Lifting a Floating Ice Cube with a Paper Clip

You will need: standard #1 medium-sized trombone paper clip, ice cube, bowl of water, salt

Form a "cradle" from a trombone paper clip by bending the outer loop down (see figure). Lay the paper clip cradle across an ice cube that is floating in a bowl of water. Put a small amount of salt on top of the part of the paper clip that is resting on the ice cube. Wait about 10 seconds; then pick up the paper clip by the top loop. The ice cube will be lifted up right along with your paper clip!

Reason: Salt lowers the freezing point of water. After the paper clip sinks into the melted part of the ice cube (melting caused by the salt), the melted water on the ice cube freezes over the top of the ice cube, trapping the paper clip. Caution: if you wait too long, the top of the ice cube will melt more completely, and the paper clip will lose its grip!

salt

Food Color Explosion

You will need: trombone paper clip, bowl of milk that has 1% to 4% fat content, food coloring, dishwashing liquid, talcum powder or pepper powder

Form a "loop cradle" out of a paper clip (see the Paper Clip Water-Drop Magnifier experiment for details). Add four drops of food coloring to the bowl of milk near the center of the bowl (one each of yellow, red, green, and blue).

Dip the paper clip cradle loop into dishwashing liquid. Touch the loop to the surface of the milk. Watch the food colors "explode" to the edges of the bowl! A similar occurrence will take place if you put pepper or talcum powder on the surface of water and then touch the surface of the water with the loop that was dipped in dishwashing liquid.

Reason: The fat in the milk holds the droplets of food coloring in one spot. However, as soon as the dishwashing liquid is added, it causes the food coloring and milk to thoroughly and rapidly mix together. The dishwashing liquid consists of molecules that have two ends: one end is "fat-friendly" (likes fat), and one end is "water-friendly."

CHEMISTRY, ELECTROCHEMISTRY, AND ELECTRICITY

Crystal Growing

You will need: paper clip; Epsom salts (magnesium sulfate),* available from a pharmacy; cooking pot; water; pencil; thread, string, or dental floss; a heat-resistant plastic jar or storage container, such as a microwaveable portion saver or a peanut butter jar; presoaked kidney bean.

Note: If you aren't allowed to use the stove yet, get a grown-up to help you with this experiment.

Tie or tape the thread to the center of the pencil. Tie the thread to the paper clip. Heat 1 cup (240 mL) of water to boiling in a cooking pot. Add Epsom salts to

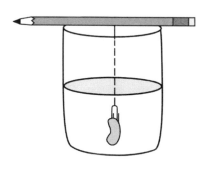

the water (or another solid; see footnote for suggestions). Stir well until all of the crystals are dissolved; they will disappear when they dissolve. Continue adding the Epsom salts or whatever solid you chose until no more dissolves. Carefully pour the hot liquid from the pot into the jar. Lower the paper clip into the liquid. The liquid should cover part of the string. Let the

---

*You can also use: salt, sugar, alum, cream of tartar, sodium carbonate (washing soda), sodium bicarbonate (baking soda), or sodium thiosulfate (available from a photographic supply store).

experiment sit overnight. Beautiful crystals will form on the clip and the thread.

If crystals do not form easily on the paper clip and thread, try the bean trick: Unbend the paper clip slightly and push a large presoaked kidney bean onto the end of the paper clip. Heat up a fresh batch of Epsom salts solution (or whatever solution you are using). Lower the bean, clip, and thread into the hot solution. Let the experiment stand overnight. Crystals should form faster and better now!

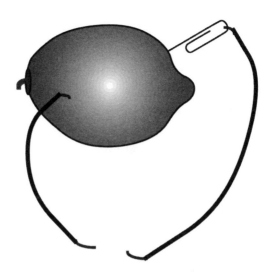

Copper- and Paper-Clip-Powered Lemon Battery

You will need: steel trombone paper clip; 2 pieces of copper wire with insulation removed from the ends; lemon; voltmeter (optional)

Twist the uncoated end of one piece of wire around a trombone paper clip's inner loop as shown. Straighten the outside end of the trombone paper clip and stick it into the lemon. Stick one end of the second piece of copper wire directly into the lemon. Touch the two loose ends of wire to your tongue. You will feel a slight tingle. What you feel on your tongue is a small amount of electricity that the lemon is producing, with help from the copper wire and the iron in the steel paper clip! (The two metals sticking into the lemon must be different in order to produce an electrical current.) If you measure the electric potential with a voltmeter, it will register about 0.2 to 0.3 volts.

You can also try aluminum foil (or an aluminum nail) in place of the paper clip, and a brass brad or thumbtack in place of the copper wire. Test with a voltmeter to see which combinations of metals provide the greatest electrical potential. Remember: the two metals in the lemon must be different from each other.

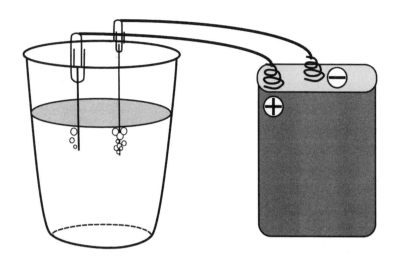

Water-Splitting

You will need: 2 trombone paper clips; 2 mechanical pencil leads; 2 copper wires, each about 1 to 2 feet (30 to 60 cm) long, with insulation removed at both ends; 6-volt lantern battery or 9-volt rectangular battery; glass of water; electrical tape or duct tape

Attach one paper clip to the end of one of the wires, and the other paper clip to the end of the other wire. Attach a pencil lead to each paper clip by slipping it between the small and large loops in the clip. Slip the paper clips over the edge of the rim of the glass, so that the pencil leads are in the water, but not touching each other. If the wires do not stay in place, tape them to the glass with small pieces of electrical tape or duct tape. Connect the free ends of the wires to the positive (+) and negative (-) electrodes of the battery as shown; do not let these wires touch.

Bubbles will quickly form on the pencil leads, because water is being split into its two atomic ingredients: hydrogen and oxygen, both of which are gases. Note that one of the electrodes (-) will give many more bubbles than the other electrode (+). This occurs because there is twice as much hydrogen as oxygen in water. (Water's formula is H_2O, which means there are two hydrogen atoms for every oxygen atom in a water molecule.) Hydrogen gas is formed as the hydrogen (+) ion picks up electrons at the negative electrode.

You may also run this experiment without the pencil leads, putting an unbent paper clip directly into the water. However, you will not see as fine a stream of bubbles. Pencil leads make better surfaces for the bubbles to form on.

Copper-Plating a Paper Clip, Using Pennies

You will need: steel trombone paper clip; 25 to 50 copper pennies* or other small copper coins; 8 to 12 ounces (240 to 360 mL) vinegar or lemon juice; jar, drinking glass, or cup of glass or plastic (it should not be made of metal)

Drop the pennies into the jar. Add the vinegar or lemon juice. Drop in the paper clip. Let the jar and its contents sit from 1 to 24 hours. Fish out the paper clip. It will be copper-coated from the copper in the pennies. The old, grungy pennies will also be shinier.

Note: If after several hours you do not see the paper clip turning a copper color, try roughing up the surface of the paper clip with steel wool, sandpaper, or with cleansing powder. You can also add some table salt to the vinegar or lemon juice to speed things up.

---

*For U.S. currency, pre-1983 pennies work best, since they have more copper in them.

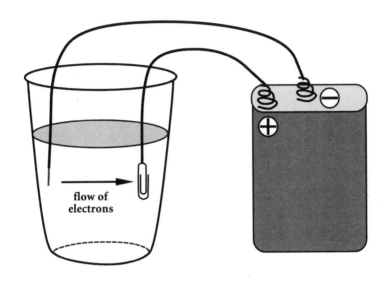

flow of electrons

Copper-Plating a Paper Clip, Using a Battery

You will need: steel trombone paper clip; two 12-inch (30-cm) lengths of plastic-coated copper bell wire; window cleaner containing ammonia; glass jar; 6-volt lantern battery; electrical tape or duct tape

Strip about 2 inches (5 cm) of insulation from both ends of both wires. Twist one end of one of the wires around the curved end of the paper clip. Hang the paper clip in the jar. Tape it in place, if necessary, to hold it. Pour window cleaner into the jar until it is about half full. Make sure that the paper clip is under the surface of the liquid. Hang one end of the second wire over the edge of the jar. Make sure that the two wires do not touch. Tape the wire to the rim of the jar if it does not stay in place. Wrap the free end of the wire that is attached to the paper clip around the positive (+) electrode of the lantern battery. Wrap the free end of the second wire around the negative (-) electrode of the lantern battery (see figure).

Bubbles should quickly start to form. Every half-hour or so, pull out the paper clip to see if it is starting to turn color. When you can finally see a color change, it shows that copper is moving from the wire through the solution, to end up plating out on the paper clip. The bubbles are caused by the splitting of water (H_2O) into the gases hydrogen (H_2) and oxygen (O_2) by the electric current. Some of the copper from the wire-end electrode is converted into copper ions and dissolves in the water. These ions migrate to the other electrode (the steel paper clip), where they are converted back to copper metal, forming a bronze-colored plating on the paper clip.

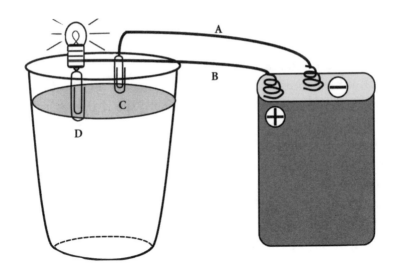

Conductivity Tester of Liquids

You will need: 2 trombone paper clips; two 12-inch (30-cm) lengths of insulated copper bell wire; liquids to be tested; glass jar; 6-volt lantern battery; flashlight bulb; electrical or duct tape

Strip about 2 inches (5 cm) of insulation from both ends of both wires. Wrap one end of one of the wires (wire *A* in the figure) around one of the paper clips. Tape this paper clip (*C*) to the inside top of the jar. Tape the second paper clip (*D*) to the inside top of the jar about an inch (2.5 cm) away; make sure that the clips do not touch. Wrap and tape an end of the second wire (wire *B*) around the grooves in a flashlight bulb, but leave the bottom unwrapped. Wrap the free end of wire *A* around one of the electrodes (terminals) of the lantern battery. Wrap the free end of wire *B* around the other electrode of the lantern battery. Pour the liquid to be tested into the jar until both paper clips are in contact with the liquid. Touch the tip of the bulb to paper clip *D*. If the bulb lights up, the liquid is a conductor of electricity. If the bulb does not light up, the liquid is a nonconductor. For weakly conducting liquids, make sure that the paper clips are close to each other.

Some liquids to try: water (poor conductor); salty water (better conductor); sugar water; water with baking soda; and other "kitchen chemicals" such as vinegar, lemon juice, orange juice, tomato juice, apple juice, club soda, grapefruit juice, milk, etc.

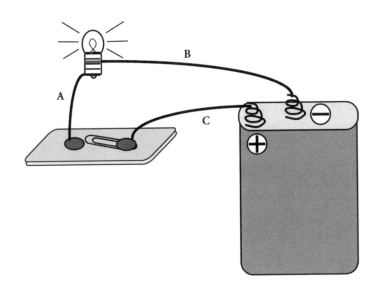

Paper Clip Light Switch

You will need: metal trombone paper clip; three 12-inch (30-cm) lengths of plastic-covered copper bell wire; 6-volt lantern battery; flashlight bulb or other small light, such as a miniature Christmas tree light bulb; tape (preferably electrical tape or duct tape); 2 metal-head thumbtacks; foam-core board, corrugated cardboard, or plywood, about 2 × 2 inches (5 × 5 cm) in size.

Strip about 1 inch (2.5 cm) of insulation from both ends of all three of the copper wires.

Tape an end of wire *A* to the bulb's metal tip. Attach the other end of wire *A* to a piece of board or plywood with a thumbtack. Tape an end of wire *B* to the bulb's metal sleeve. Connect the other end of wire *B* to one of the lantern battery terminals.

Attach one end of wire *C* to a piece of board with a

thumbtack, tacking a paper clip under it; make sure that the paper clip is able to move freely. The paper clip should be near enough to the first tack to be able to touch it when the clip is rotated. Connect the other end of wire *C* to the other lantern battery terminal.

Swing the paper clip back and forth. When the paper clip touches tack *A*, the light will turn *on*. When the clip does not touch the tack, the light will be *off*. You've just made a light switch!

MAGNETISM

Paper Clip Magnetic Strength Tester

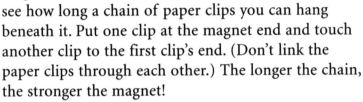

You will need: about a dozen uncoated metal trombone paper clips; several magnets; piece of aluminum foil
2 × 2 inches (5 × 5 cm); steel butter knife

Let's see how strong various magnets are. Choose one of your magnets. Hold up the magnet and see how long a chain of paper clips you can hang beneath it. Put one clip at the magnet end and touch another clip to the first clip's end. (Don't link the paper clips through each other.) The longer the chain, the stronger the magnet!

Slip a piece of aluminum foil between the magnet and the clips. The clips will stay attached. However, when a steel knife blade is placed between the magnet and the clips, the clips will fall. Iron or steel interrupts the magnet's attraction (its magnetic field), but aluminum does not.

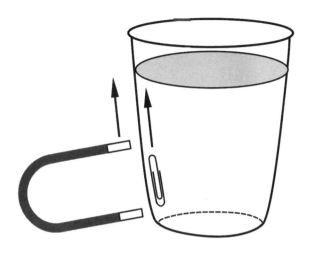

Retrieving a Paper Clip in Water

You will need: paper clip, strong magnet, glass of water

Drop a paper clip into a glass of water. How do you get it out without getting your hands wet? Simple! Just hold a strong magnet on the bottom of the glass near the paper clip.

When the magnet is close enough to the paper clip, the clip will be attracted to the magnet and will move up against the inside of the glass. Slowly raise the magnet up the side of the glass. The paper clip will rise also. When you get to the top of the glass, the paper clip will hop onto the magnet, and your hands will still be dry!

Magic Magnetic Paper Clip

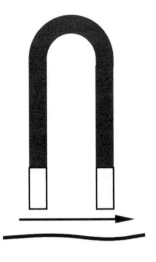

You will need: steel paper clip, strong permanent magnet

Straighten out a paper clip. Rub it in *one* direction (*not* back and forth) about 20 to 30 times with a strong magnet. You now have turned your paper clip into a magnet! When you touch this straightened-out magnetic paper clip to other paper clips, it will attract them!

You can also do this trick with other pieces of iron or steel, such as scissors. However, unless the piece of iron or steel has been hardened, or is a special alloy, it will lose its magnetism, unlike the strong permanent magnet.

More fun: Try turning other objects into magnets, such as a fork, spoon, or a tableware knife. All it takes is a strong magnet and several dozen rubs in one direction along the metal surface of the object you want to magnetize.

Paper Clip Compass

You will need: small paper clip; piece of cardboard or foam-core board; dish of water; high-strength magnet

Bend a paper clip back and forth until you've broken off a straight piece. Rub the piece vigorously and many times (about 40 to 100 times) in one direction with one pole (end) of a high-strength magnet.

Cut out a square or circle of cardboard or foam-core board about ¾ to 1 inch (2 to 2.5 cm) across. Place the paper clip piece in the center of the board. Float the board piece in a small dish of water. When a magnet is placed near the board, the paper clip will turn until it points to the magnet. If no magnet is nearby, the magnetized paper clip piece will point in the north–south direction of the Earth's magnetic field, thus acting as a compass.

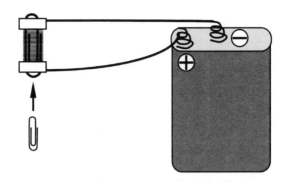

Paper Clip Electromagnet

You will need: jumbo trombone paper clip, small paper clip, enamel-coated 30-gauge (small diameter) insulated magnet wire, tape, 6-volt lantern battery

Leaving a 12-inch (30.5 cm) length of wire hanging free at the start, wrap magnet wire 100 times around a jumbo paper clip. Tape the wire near the end of the paper clip. Leave about 12 inches (30 cm) of wire hanging free at the outer end. Scrape off about 1 inch (2.5 cm) of the wire's enamel insulation from each end of the wire, using a penknife.

Attach the two wire ends to the terminals of a 6-volt lantern battery. Electricity will flow through the wire and around the jumbo paper clip, turning it into an electromagnet, which will pick up small iron objects. Try lifting up a small paper clip with your electromagnet. (Be careful not to keep the wires hooked up for too long a time to the battery; the wire will get hot from the electricity going through it.)

When you disconnect the wires from the battery, your jumbo paper clip will keep some of its magnetism for a short period of time.

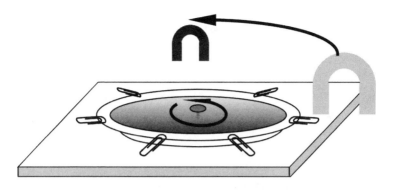

Paper Clip Plate Spinner Motor (Magnetic Spinning Clipsplate)

You will need: The spinning clipsplate described earlier in this book [a small plate works best, about 4 to 7 inches (10 to 18 cm) in diameter]; piece of corrugated cardboard or foam-core board bigger than the plate; thumbtack; magnet

Push a thumbtack through the center of the clipsplate, into the foam-core board or cardboard. Slowly move the magnet in a circle around the edge of the plate. The plate will turn because of the attraction that the paper clips have to the magnet.

Paper Clip Magnetic Flower

You will need: six colored paper clips; six long pipe cleaners; magnet; bar of soap, tape

You can make a flower that opens and closes. Twist 6 pipe cleaners together at one end, leaving a little of the ends sticking out at the side. Continue twisting them together halfway up the shafts. Stick the twisted ends into a bar of soap; use green soap for "pretend" grass. Spread out the upper parts of the pipe cleaners. Twist each upper end around a colored paper clip and tape it in place. These will be the petals of your "flower."

Lower a magnet into the middle of the paper clips. Watch the paper clips petals surge toward the magnet, closing the flower! To reopen the flower, simply withdraw the magnet. If the paper clips do not move very much, bend the pipe cleaners closer to each other.

To make the flower look even more lifelike, tape pieces of paper cut in the shape of flower petals to each paper clip.

Paper Clips and Clip Critters Suspended in Space

You will need: paper clips, strong magnet, construction paper, thread, tape, aluminum foil, steel fork or spoon, scissors

Tape one end of a foot-long (30-cm) piece of thread to a paper clip. Tape down the other end to a table top. Touch a strong magnet to the paper clip. Gradually raise the magnet until the thread becomes taut (tight). Then, ever so slowly, raise the magnet until the paper clip seems to "float" in air just below the magnet.

Cut out birds, bats, butterflies, snakes, elephants, mice, flowers, trees, watermelons, kites, planes, flying saucers, etc., from construction paper, and tape paper clips to each of them. Attach one end of a thread to the paper clip on the critter and the other end to the table. Watch each critter become suspended in air when a magnet is brought near it. What happens when you place a piece of paper between the magnet and the suspended things? How about a piece of aluminum foil or a steel fork, knife, or spoon from the dinner table?

Spinning Suspended Paper Clip on a Straw

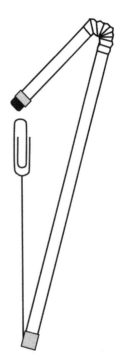

You will need: trombone paper clip, small button magnet, flexible drinking straw, plastic tape, thread

Tape a small button magnet into the short end of a flexible straw (see figure). Tape one end of a 6-inch (15 cm) piece of thread to the other end of the straw. Tie the free end of the thread to a small paper clip.

Bend the straw until the paper clip barely touches the magnet. Now *ever so slowly* pull the ends of the straw away from each other, so that the paper clip is no longer touching the magnet, but is still held in its magnetic "grasp." Tape a small piece of plastic tape around the bend of the straw to hold the straw in place at the desired angle.

Turn the straw vertically, slightly tilted so that the paper clip and thread are pointed up and down (see figure). If you gently tap the paper clip on its side, it will spin, while still being held within the magnetic field.

Fish Rescue from Evil Paper Clip Octopus

You will need: stiff construction paper or an index card, 32 medium-sized paper clips, jumbo trombone paper clip, magnet, 32 brass paper fasteners, 8 × 8 inch (20 × 20 cm) piece of cardboard or foam-core board, tape, and a paper clip fish. See the Paper Clip Fishing Game for instructions on making a fish.

Cut an oval octopus head from construction paper about 4 inches (10 cm) wide. Place the head on a piece of foam-core board or cardboard. Push two paper fasteners through the head of the octopus for eyes. Draw a mouth.

Make eight arms (tentacles), using four paper clips per arm. Push a paper fastener through each paper clip link in the arms, and spread apart the fastener's points. Attach a claw (an unbent jumbo trombone paper clip) to one of the arms. Tape one end of each of the arms to the octopus's head. Hook the claw through your fish's paper clip. Without touching the fish, use a magnet to rescue the fish from the octopus's clutches. Can you do it more quickly when the magnet is above, or below, the board?

Dancing Dolls

You will need: construction paper or three 3 × 5 inch (7.5 × 12.5 cm) index cards; 3 small trombone paper clips; a magnet; an aluminum or glass pie pan; scissors; tracing paper; glue; pencil

Cut out dolls from the cards or from construction paper. They should be about 4 or 5 inches tall (10 or 12.5 cm). Bend the bottom inch of each doll at a right angle and fasten a paper clip to it.

Place the dolls on an inverted (upside-down) aluminum or pie pan. Put a magnet underneath the pan. As you move the magnet around, the dolls will dance! Cut out and create a whole group of colorful dancers.

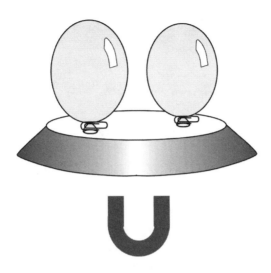

Dancing Balloons

You will need: 2 small balloons, 2 trombone paper clips, a magnet, an aluminum or glass pie pan

Create magnetic "dancing" balloons! Blow up (inflate) some small balloons, about 3 to 5 inches (7.5 to 12.5 cm) in diameter. Twist each balloon end to keep the air from leaking out and seal the ends with paper clips. There's no need to have to tie off the end of the balloons; it's much simpler to use paper clips! Place one or more balloons on the bottom of an inverted pie pan. Move a magnet underneath. The balloons will move and dance!

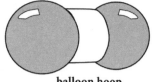

with one clip   with two clips

balloon hoop

Paper Clip Hoop Race

You will need: 5 × 8 inch (12.5 × 20 cm) index card or piece of stiff construction paper; 2 to 4 medium-sized trombone paper clips; magnet; 2 small round balloons, 3 to 5 inches (7.5 to 12.5 cm) in diameter; tape

Cut an index card in half down its long dimension. You now have two pieces of 8-inch-long (20-cm) cards, each 2½ inches (6.5 cm) wide. Tape the narrow ends of each piece together to make a hoop about 2½ inches (6.5 cm) in diameter. Tape a paper clip to the inside center of one hoop. Make a second hoop. Tape two paper clips to the inside of it, on opposite sides of the hoop. Which hoop rolls better? The hoop with only one clip is not balanced, and is harder to roll.

Try propelling the hoop by holding a magnet just in front of it. If it is hard to keep the hoop from jumping onto the magnet, try adding balloons! Blow up two small round balloons. Tie them off and tape them to the ends of the hoop. Your "balloon hoop" will now be much better behaved. This is because the balloons have better traction on the table than paper, are rounder, and roll more easily. You will also now be able to tape paper clips on the *outside* of the hoop, which will make it easier for the magnet to pull.

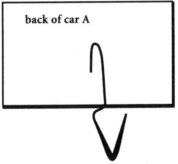

back of car A

Paper Clip Race Cars

You will need: two 3 × 5 inch (7.5 × 12.5 cm) index
cards or pieces of oak tag, or pieces of stiff construction paper, jumbo trombone paper clips, magnet,
scissors, tape, aluminum pan

Cut out a 3 × 5 inch (7.5 × 12.5 cm) piece of oak
tag or construction paper, or use an index card that
size. Draw a racing car *(A)* on it, or trace the one in
the picture. Bend a paper clip at right angles and tape
it to the car. Put your car on a nonmagnetic surface,
such as an aluminum pan. Hold a magnet below the

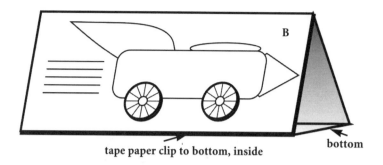

tape paper clip to bottom, inside   **bottom**

surface of your race track to make your cars move!

Draw a line 1 inch (2.5 cm) in from and parallel to each long side of a 3 × 5 inch index card or stiff paper that size. Another way to make a magnetic race car: fold the 3 × 5 inch piece of paper or card into a triangular shape along the lines as shown in *B;* tape the sides in place if necessary.

Draw pictures of a car on the two upright sides, and tape a paper clip to the inside bottom of the folded shape. Run your car (car *B*) in the same way you ran car *A.*

Paper Clip Fishing Game

You will need: two colors of construction paper or 10 small index cards (3 × 5 inches or 7.5 × 12.5 cm); 20 small trombone paper clips; two magnets (horseshoe magnets work best); string or thread; bowl of water; two empty paper towel rolls (or rods, such as wooden dowels); tape; crayon; scissors

This is a game for two people. Make a fishing rod by taping a foot-long (30 cm) piece of string to one end of an empty paper towel roll or a rod. Tie a magnet to the other end of the string. Make another fishing rod the same way for your partner. Cut pieces of construction paper in the shape of fish. Make 10 fish of one color, and 10 fish of another color. If you use white index cards, color half the fish with a crayon.

Clip a paper clip onto the nose of each fish. Fill a large bowl halfway with water. Put the fish into the water, one at a time, alternating the different colors; it doesn't matter whether the fish sink or float. Have a race to see who can remove all of his/her fish from the bowl using only a fishing rod! Each person fishes for one color of fish.

TRICKS
Spool Car

You will need: a large (jumbo) trombone paper clip, a medium-sized trombone paper clip, spool of thread about 1¼ inches (3 cm) in diameter, with or without thread, tape, two rubber bands

Push one end of a rubber band through the hole in a spool of thread; if you have difficulty, push it through with a straightened-out paper clip. When one end of the rubber band pokes out of the far end of the spool, slip it onto a medium-sized paper clip. Tape the paper clip to the far end of the spool.

Slip the rubber band at the near end of the spool through a large (jumbo) paper clip; turn this clip with your finger to wind it. Pull on the rubber band as needed in order to get it to stretch to fit into the spool; otherwise, the rubber band tends to bunch up.

After the rubber band is twisted into the hole, keep winding for about 20 to 30 additional turns. Release the spool car. It will dash across the floor or table top! If the car slips a little, just wrap a rubber band around the center of the spool to give it more traction.

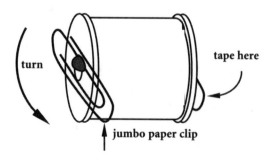

Magic Rollback Can

You will need: 2 trombone paper clips; 2 large rubber bands; a round container with a plastic lid (such as a nut can, snack food can, or coffee can); a heavy metal washer (or nut and bolt); nail; hammer

Poke a hole in the top (plastic lid) and bottom of

Attachment of rubber bands on the washer.

the can by hammering the nail through it. Get an adult to help you if necessary. Thread the rubber bands onto a large washer. Push one of the rubber bands through the hole in the bottom of the can; use the point of a pencil or pen to help push the rubber band into the hole. After you pull the rubber band end out through the hole, attach a paper clip to it to keep it from being pulled back in. Push the end of the second rubber band through the hole in the lid and secure it with the second paper clip.

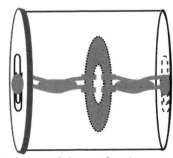

Position of the washer in can.

Put the lid onto the can. Roll the can away from you. Like a faithful dog, it will return to you! If your can happens to act somewhat lazy and does not want to return as energetically as you'd like it to, try this "fix": prewind the can by rotating the paper clip *before* you set the can on the ground. When you push the can away from you, it will roll back better.

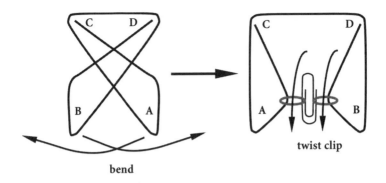

bend

twist clip

Paper Clip/Rubber Band Envelope Surprise

You will need: butterfly paper clip; small trombone paper clip; envelope; 2 small rubber bands

Bend the butterfly paper clip as shown, pulling the loops (*A* and *B*) outward until they are past each other. Attach small rubber bands to the outside edges of a small paper clip; make sure that the rubber band is connected to the *sides* of the paper clip as shown, and not to the outer and middle loops. Attach the rubber bands to loops *A* and *B* of your butterfly clip (see the figure).

Twist the small paper clip around itself in a circle many times, until the rubber bands are tight. Then slip the Paper Clip/Rubber Band Surprise into an envelope. Mail it to a friend that you want to surprise. When the friend opens the envelope, the Paper Clip/Rubber Band Envelope Surprise will jump around and make noise! For additional fun, you can also hide the surprise under a book. What a surprise for the next person who picks it up!

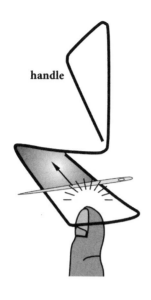

handle

Soap Film Rolls a Needle

You will need: one butterfly paper clip, sewing needle or round toothpick, water, dishwashing liquid, bowl

Bend the butterfly paper clip as shown to make a bubble wand (see the Paper Clip Bubble Wand experiment in this book for bending directions). Hold the wand so the handle is vertical and the loop is horizontal. Dip the wand into a bowl containing 1 part dishwashing liquid and 10 parts water so a film of soap bubble forms in the wand. Place a needle or round toothpick across the middle of the loop. (The bubble wand handle is vertical at this time.)

Slowly lift up the wand, keeping the film intact and keeping the needle or toothpick in the middle of the loop. Gently poke one side of the soap film bubble with your finger and pop it. The unpopped soap film on the other side of the needle will jerk the needle off to one side! This occurs because the soap film, wanting to stick together, pulls with equal force on all sides of the bubble wand. When the film is broken (popped) with your finger, the force on one side suddenly is decreased. The needle or toothpick is pulled right off the edge of the frame by the force on the remaining sides.

Pushing a Paper Clip into a Balloon without Popping It

You will need: one medium or small trombone paper clip; balloon; 2-inch-wide (5-cm) clear packaging tape

Straighten the outer bend in the paper clip as shown in the figure. Inflate a good-quality round balloon and tie it off. Tape a 2 × 2 inch (5 × 5 cm) piece of clear packaging tape to the balloon. Push the straightened end of the paper clip through the patch of tape into the balloon. The balloon will not pop! Instead, it will gradually leak air around the hole where the paper clip is embedded.

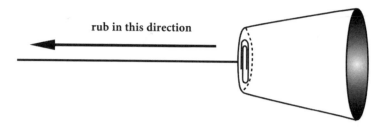

rub in this direction

Squawking Cup

You will need: paper cup; cotton string; two medium-sized trombone paper clips; waxed paper

Poke a small hole in the bottom center of a paper cup; to make the hole, you can use either a ballpoint pen or a partially straightened paper clip

Push one end of a piece of cotton string through the hole from the outside in. Tie the inner end of string to a paper clip. Gently pull on the string until the paper clip rests against the inside bottom of the cup.

Pull the outside end of the string tight with one hand, away from the bottom of the cup. Slowly rub along the string with the other hand. Wet your rubbing hand to get a louder sound. Listen to the cup make strange squawking noises! To get a different sound, try dragging some waxed paper along the string between your fingers.

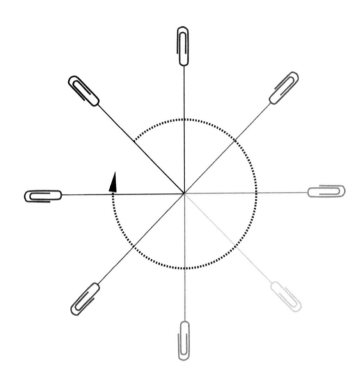

Whistling Paper Clip

You will need: jumbo trombone paper clip; 1-foot-long (30-cm) string

Tie a jumbo paper clip to the end of a 1-foot-long (30-cm) piece of string. Swing the string over your head in a circle at arm's length, being careful not to hit anything or anyone.

When the paper clip is swung fast enough, it will make a whistling sound. The sound is caused by the movement of air through the paper clip. Another example of sound created by air moving past objects is the "wind noise" you hear when you ride in an automobile with a window open.

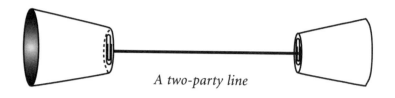

A two-party line

Paper Clip and Cup Party Telephone Line

You will need: 4 paper clips ; 2 pieces of string, each 3 to 6 feet (90 to 180 cm) long; 4 paper cups

Two-party line: Punch a hole in the bottom center of two paper cups. Push an end of a 3- to 6-foot long (90 to 180 cm) piece of string through the hole in each of two cups from the outside to the inside, making sure that the open ends of the cups are facing away from each other). Inside each cup, tie a paper clip to the string end. Pull the cups taut (tight) and speak into one. A person listening at the other end will hear you through the string.

Four-party line: To have a four-way party line, make another set of phones in the same way you made the two-person party line. Connect them to the center of the first set you made. Now you and up to three of your friends can have a party-line talk on your own personal telephone system!

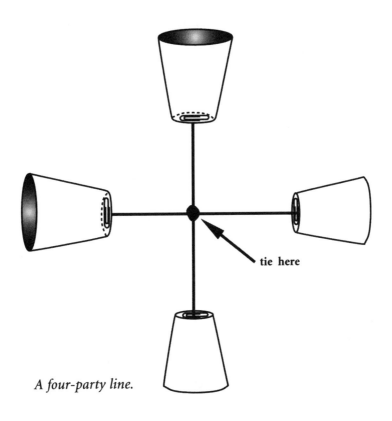

tie here

A four-party line.

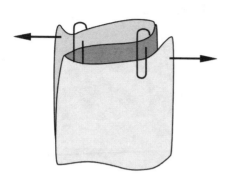

Paper Clips' Magic Dollar Bill Link

You will need: Two medium paper clips; dollar bill or other paper money

Fold a dollar bill into an S shape. Fasten one of the paper clips over one of the ends of the bill and the center fold (see drawing). Fasten the other paper clip over the other end in the same way. Each clip must pinch together two (and not three) thicknesses of the dollar bill. Make sure that the paper clips pinch the bill as shown in the drawing. Grasp one end of the bill with one hand and the other end of the bill with your other hand. Pull quickly. The paper clips will pop off the bill, linked together! (Without your touching the paper clips, they have magically linked themselves together with a simple flick of your wrists!)

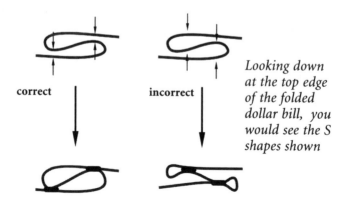

correct   incorrect

Looking down at the top edge of the folded dollar bill, you would see the S shapes shown

Index

Metric Conversion

Into Metric Units	Out of Metric Units
LENGTH	**LENGTH**
1 inch = 2.54 centimeters	1 millimeter = 0.04 inch
1 foot = 30 centimeters	1 centimeter = 0.4 inch
1 yard = 0.9 meters	1 meter = 3.3 feet
MASS (WEIGHT)	**MASS (WEIGHT)**
1 ounce = 28 grams	1 gram = 0.035 ounces
1 pound = 0.45 kilograms	1 kilogram = 2.2 pounds
VOLUME	**VOLUME**
1 teaspoon = 5 milliliters	1 milliliter = 0.03 fluid ounces
1 tablespoon = 15 milliliters	5 milliliters = 1 teaspoon
1 fluid ounce = 30 milliliters	15 milliliters = 1 tablespoon
1 cup = 0.24 liters	240 milliliters = 1 cup
or 240 milliliters	1 liter = 2.1 pints
ABBREVIATIONS	**ABBREVIATIONS**
in = inches	cm = centimeters
ft = feet	mL = milliliters